Natalie Jean
and
The FLYING MACHINE

by Kersten Hamilton
pictures by Susan Harrison

Tyndale House Publishers
Wheaton, Illinois

Library of Congress Cataloging-in-Publication Data

Hamilton, K. R. (Kersten R.)
    Natalie Jean and the flying machine / by Kersten Hamilton ;
pictures by Susan Harrison.
        p.   cm. — (Natalie Jean adventures ; bk. 1)
    Summary: When she breaks her sister's favorite doll, Natalie Jean
turns to Jesus for guidance.
    ISBN 0-8423-4620-1 (pbk.)
    [1. Forgiveness — Fiction.   2. Christian life — Fiction.]
I. Harrison, Susan, ill.   II. Title.   III. Series: Hamilton, K. R.
(Kersten R.).   Natalie Jean adventures ; bk. 1.
PZ7.H1824Nau   1991   90-72050
[E] — dc20

Book development by March Media, Inc., Brentwood, Tennessee

Printed in the United States of America

98   97   96   95   94   93   92   91
 9   8   7   6   5   4   3   2   1

CONTENTS

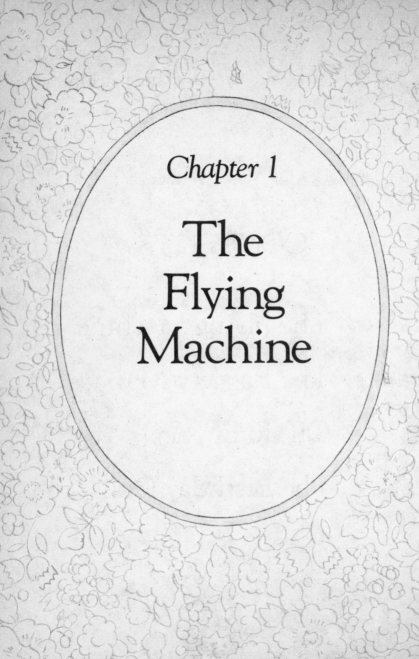

Chapter 1

The Flying Machine

"Natalie Jean's famous flying machine
is ready to fly," said Natalie.
She set her sister Tessa's favorite doll,
Lucinda, in the pilot's seat.
"Stand back, Samson," she said.
"Meow," said Samson.

Natalie tossed the flying machine out
the window.
"Fly, fly!" she called.
The machine flew straight down to the
ground.
Lucinda flew straight down to the ground
too, and smashed to smithereens.

Natalie looked at the broken doll.
"I have broken Tessa's favorite doll," she
said.
She put her hands over her eyes.
"Tessa is going to be mad.
I am not supposed to play with her doll.
Jesus is going to be sad.
What am I going to do, Samson?"
"Meow," said Samson.

Natalie pulled the pillowslip off her pillow and hid it under her petticoat. Then she went downstairs.

Tessa was sitting on the bottom step looking at pictures in a book.

"What are you doing, Natalie?" she asked.

"Nothing," Natalie said.

"Can I do nothing with you?" Tessa asked.

"No," said Natalie. "I want to do nothing alone."

Natalie hurried out the door.
She found Lucinda and the flying
machine behind a rosebush.

Natalie carefully picked up all the broken
pieces.
She put them in the pillowslip.
Then she shoved the pillowslip under
her petticoat.
It made her look fat.
The broken pieces went *clink, clink*
when she walked.
The bag kept trying to slip down.
Natalie took two steps—*shuffle, shuffle.*
Then *hop,* she had to pull the bag back up.

When Natalie came back to the front
door, Tessa was standing on the porch.
"Why are you walking like that?" she
asked.
"It is a new game," said Natalie.
Tessa started to follow Natalie.
She did the shuffle-hop too.

"Why are you following me?" asked
  Natalie.
"I want to play the new game,"
  said Tessa. "How are you making that
  funny noise when you hop?"
"I am not making a funny noise,"
  said Natalie.

"Yes, you are," said Tessa. "You go
    tinkle, tinkle when you hop."
"You are too young to play this game,"
    Natalie said. "Go away."
"No," said Tessa. "I can hop just as high
    as you can."
    Natalie shuffle-hopped very fast.
    Tessa shuffle-hopped behind her.
    Samson ran behind Tessa.
"Hurray!" said Tessa. "We have
    a parade!"

Natalie shuffle-hopped around the house faster.

Tessa was still behind her.

When Natalie came to the porch, she stopped.

"This game has a new rule," she said.

"The rule is, you stay here."

"I do not like that rule," said Tessa.

"A rule is a rule," said Natalie. "Are you going to play or not?"

"Yes, I am," said Tessa.

She sat down.

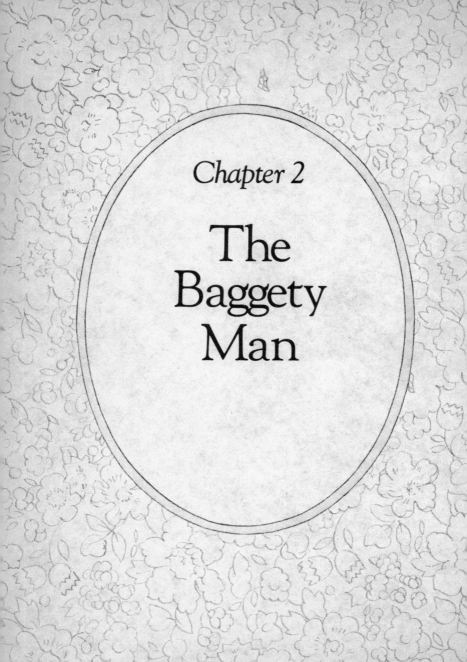

Chapter 2

The Baggety Man

Natalie did the shuffle-hop around the
corner.
She shuffle-hopped out the back gate.
Then she took the pillowslip out from
under her skirt and hid it in the
woodpile.

"That is the end of that," Natalie said. She picked Samson up.

"We are the only ones who will ever know what happened to Lucinda, Samson," she said.

She knew that was not true.

Jesus knew about Lucinda.

But Natalie Jean did not want to talk to him.

"I am done with that game," Natalie said when she came back to the porch.

"Good," Tessa said. "Let's have a doll party."

"No!" Natalie said. "I do not want to play dolls today. Let's swing."

Natalie and Tessa both sat on the big
swing.
They pumped their legs back and forth,
back and forth.
The swing went higher and higher.
"I can see over the fence!" Tessa called.
Natalie looked over the fence.
She could see the woodpile.
Swoosh, they came back down.
Natalie felt as if her tummy stayed at
the top.

"We are swinging too high," she said.
"My tummy does not like it. Let the
swing stop, and I will tell you a story."

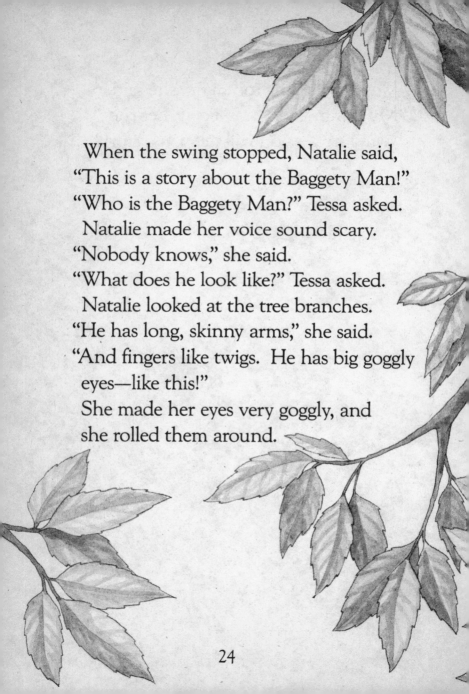

When the swing stopped, Natalie said,
"This is a story about the Baggety Man!"
"Who is the Baggety Man?" Tessa asked.
  Natalie made her voice sound scary.
"Nobody knows," she said.
"What does he look like?" Tessa asked.
  Natalie looked at the tree branches.
"He has long, skinny arms," she said.
"And fingers like twigs. He has big goggly
  eyes—like this!"
She made her eyes very goggly, and
  she rolled them around.

"But the scary thing about the Baggety
  Man is his shoes!"

"What about his shoes?" Tessa asked.
"Maybe I should not tell you. Maybe you
  are too little."
"I am *not* too little!" Tessa yelled.
"Shhhh," said Natalie. "He might hear
  you."
"The Baggety Man?" Tessa asked.
  She looked over her shoulder.
"Yes," said Natalie. "The Baggety Man.
  He has shoes that go bounce, bounce,
  bounce as high as a house."

"That is not very scary," said Tessa.

"The Baggety Man bounces all around town, looking for open windows," said Natalie.

"Oh," said Tessa. "What does he do when he finds one?"

"He bounces inside," Natalie said. "He bounces on the bed. He bounces on the floor. Then he takes out his bag!"

"Oh, no!" cried Tessa. "Not his bag!"

"Oh, yes," Natalie said. "And—he grabs them!"

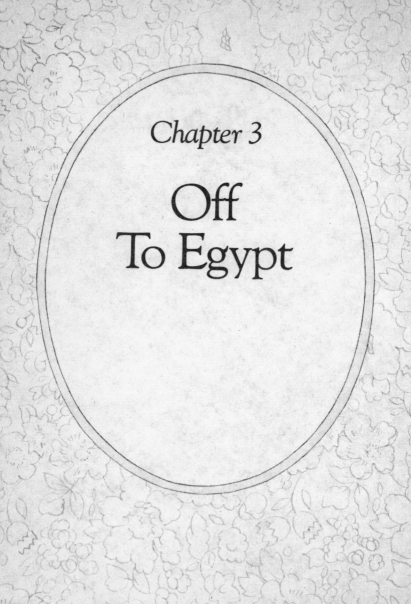

Chapter 3

Off
To Egypt

"What does he grab, Natalie? What?"
Tessa asked.

"Dolls! He grabs dolls!"

"I don't believe you!" said Tessa.

"Oh, dear," said Natalie. "Look at the
window to our bedroom! It is open!"
Tessa jumped off the swing.
She ran to the back door and rushed
inside.

Natalie followed her up the stairs.
Tessa looked at her bed.
Lucinda was not there.

"It is true, Natalie," she said. "The Baggety
Man is true!"
She ran out of the room.
Natalie saw a tear on her face as she
ran past.
"Tessa, come back," she called.
But Tessa ran down the stairs.

Natalie sat down.
Samson looked at her.
He twitched his tail.
"I do not feel happy, Samson," she said.
"First, I took Lucinda. Then I told a lie.
If I had a flying machine, I would get in
it and fly away."

Samson did not say anything.
Natalie pulled her carpetbag out from
under her bed.

"I *am* going to run away," she said.

"I will go to Alaska. I can build an igloo
to live in."

"Meow?" asked Samson.

"You are right. I do not like snow. I will go
to Egypt and live with the camels."

Samson did not say anything.

Natalie stuffed her green scarf in her
carpetbag.
She put on her straw bonnet and tied it
under her chin.
"This will keep the hot sun off my head,"
she said.
"Meow?" asked Samson.
"Of course you can come with me,"
said Natalie.

She shut her carpetbag.
"Good-by, bedroom," she said. "Good-by,
soft pillow. I will sleep on a rock from
now on."
She opened the door.
Then she stopped.
She could hear Tessa crying.

Chapter 4

The Birthday Doll

Natalie shook her head.

"Tessa's heart is breaking, Samson," she said.
"It is all my fault. Running away is not
going to fix Lucinda. And it will not make
Tessa feel better. I do not know what to do.
I need help."

Then Natalie remembered something her
mother had told her.

"Jesus will help you," her mother had said, "even if you make him sad."

Natalie knelt down.

"Jesus," she said, "I need help. I am sorry I made you sad. I am sorry I played with Lucinda without asking Tessa. I am sorry I said the Baggety Man took her doll. Please help me find a way to make it better."

When Natalie opened her eyes, she saw her birthday doll.

It had golden curls and eyes that opened and shut.

Natalie had an idea.

She took her doctor's bag out of the closet
and put in bandages and a bottle of glue.
She put on a white apron with a red cross
on it, just like a real nurse.
Then she went to the woodpile to find
the pillowslip.
"This patient is not in good shape, Samson,"
she said.
"Meow," said Samson.

First Natalie glued Lucinda's head back together.

Then she tied a white bandage around it.

She glued the fingers back on Lucinda's hand.

She wrapped it in a white bandage.

"There," said Natalie. "Now comes the hardest part, Samson."

Natalie took Lucinda to Tessa.

She brought her birthday doll too.

"The Baggety Man did not steal Lucinda," Natalie said. "I threw her out the window in my flying machine."

Tessa looked sad.

She held Lucinda close.

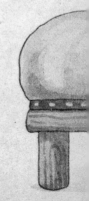

"I am on my way to Egypt to live with the
camels," Natalie said. "I want you to have
my birthday doll before I go—to keep."
Natalie left the dolls with Tessa.
She picked up her carpetbag, her bonnet,
and Samson.

Sadly, she walked out the door.
She walked to the front gate.
Then she heard someone calling her.
"Natalie!" Tessa called. "Natalie, wait! I do not want you to go to Egypt," she said. "I would miss you too much. We can share the birthday doll."

"Did you hear that, Samson?" Natalie
asked. "Jesus helped me! It's going to be
all right!"

"Meow," said Samson.